DUCK, DIVE,
ROCK & ROLL

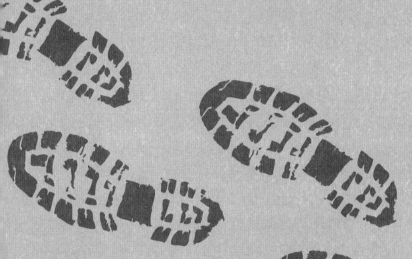

BY KENNY ABDO

ILLUSTRATED BY BOB DOUCET

magic wagon

visit us at www.abdopublishing.com

Published by Magic Wagon, a division of the ABDO Group,
PO Box 398166, Minneapolis, Minnesota 55439. Copyright © 2014
by Abdo Consulting Group, Inc. International copyrights reserved in all
countries. All rights reserved. No part of this book may be reproduced
in any form without written permission from the publisher.

Calico Chapter Books™ is a trademark and logo of Magic Wagon.

Printed in the United States of America, North Mankato, Minnesota.
062013
092013

 This book contains at least 10% recycled materials.

Text by Kenny Abdo
Illustrations by Bob Doucet
Edited by Karen Latchana Kenney
Cover and interior design by Colleen Dolphin, Mighty Media, Inc.

Library of Congress Cataloging-in-Publication Data
Abdo, Kenny, 1986-
  Duck, dive, rock & roll / Kenny Abdo ; illustrated by Bob Doucet.
      p. cm. – (Haven't got a clue!)
  Summary: Immediately after switching schools, Jon Gummyshoes,
fourth-grade detective, is confronted with a new case–someone is trying
to sabotage one of the bands in the upcoming Battle of the Bands by
threatening the lead singer.
  ISBN 978-1-61641-952-3
1. Bands (Music)–Juvenile fiction. 2. Music–Competitions–Juvenile
fiction. 3. Threats–Juvenile fiction. 4. Elementary schools–Juvenile
fiction. [1. Mystery and detective stories. 2. Bands (Music)–Fiction. 3.
Contests–Fiction. 4. Threats–Fiction. 5. Elementary schools–Fiction. 6.
Schools–Fiction.] I. Doucet, Bob, ill. II. Title. III. Title: Duck, dive, rock
and roll.
  PZ7.A1589334Duc 2013
  813.6–dc23
                                        2013001067

Table of Contents

The Usual Suspects
THE WHO'S WHO OF THE CASE

JON
GUMMYSHOES

LAWRENCE
"LARRY"
MACGUFFIN

BECKY
LIPGLOSS

JAROD
O'BERRY

JIMMY
BLUES

HUNTER
BLATZ

5

Note from the Detective's Files

The name is Gummyshoes—Jon Gummyshoes. I know what you're thinking: funny name, right? Well, that's not what I'm here to talk about. I'm here to tell you the facts. The cold, hard facts about the cases I come across day in and day out at Edwin West Elementary School.

The way I see it, trouble seems to find me around every corner. So I make it my business to clean it up. I don't need this game. It needs me.

The case I'm about to share with you wasn't my first, and it certainly won't be my last. It took me in a new direction. I had to deal with a new school, a new principal, and even a rock band. It was pretty crazy—wild bike chases, strange threats, and bodyguard duty. In the end, I learned that being a star isn't all that it's cracked up to be.

CHAPTER 1
A Shooting Star

My vision was blurry. I was trying to keep the sweat from getting into my eyes, but it wasn't working. The houses faded behind me with each turn of my bike pedals. The brilliant oranges and reds of the trees blurred as I sped by. I could see my breath as I rode the bike up the hill. Fake skeletons and cotton spider webs were all over the houses. Soon youngsters in costumes would come out to collect candy. This year would be the first year in my ten-year-old life that I wouldn't be joining them.

My bike passenger was squeezing my stomach a little too tightly. It was hard to keep going. But I had to push on, faster and faster. The Battle of the Bands and the fate of everyone involved depended on it.

See, I had decided to try my detective work at a new school for a while. I moved my operation to Edwin East. But they didn't really like the idea of a student detective there. They thought I was out to get them. But really, I was out to help them. That's what got me where I was—on my bike.

I turned onto Jugg Street and pedaled through crowds of people strolling along the sidewalk. I weaved and screamed trying to get them out of my way. I rode off the sidewalk and pedaled harder across the street.

Huffing and puffing, I felt the burn in my chest become more and more intense. My legs were tensing up and I felt like they would go up in flames. I reached the main gate and a poster by the entrance read "Edwin East's Battle of

the Bands! Featuring Hearts Not Farts! Tonight only!"

Past the sign, I saw a large crowd. Wait—not crowd, it was a mob. They were waiting by the entrance, wild with excitement. But I was headed for the Dumpster. I expertly avoided the crowd through the side entrance. We skidded to a stop by the Dumpster without anyone seeing us.

Next, we had to climb into the Dumpster and wait. MacGuffin, my partner and best pal, was going to give the all clear. Now, a Dumpster isn't my idea of a great place to spend some time. But, it was all part of the plan—the plan to deliver Edwin East's shooting star.

CHAPTER 2
Through the Mob

Let's back up to the beginning. Yesterday, I arrived at Edwin East Elementary School to find a group of students surrounding Principal Ant. He was trying to calm them down.

"Principal Ant, you can't be serious!" a girl shouted. Another student mumbled, "Edwin East will feel like a prison with a detective here."

"Listen, guys," Principal Ant said, gesturing to the students. He pointed at the girl who shouted, "especially you, Olivia. He's a detective, but he won't be watching your every move. You understand?"

He seemed like a good guy. *Hopefully we won't have to butt heads with each other,* I thought. That usually made the cases go a little more smoothly.

If I was going to make a good impression with my teachers, then I could not be late to class. If I didn't want to be late, I'd have to walk through a sea of people. That sea was filled with people who wanted to see me hanging from a flagpole by my underpants. I raised my hand to cover my face and started walking.

"Yeah, this Gumshoes guy sounds like a real bozo!" I said, trying to walk past the group.

"A real bozo!" Olivia Pumpernickel agreed. She didn't even notice me as I walked by.

Olivia reminded me of certain students back at Edwin West. I had only seen her a few times, but I had a pretty good read on her. She was the typical overachieving type, if you know what I mean. She wore a three-tone pink jumper that was probably laid out the night before. It had been ironed to perfection. She had received straight As for every semester of her academic career. She was either going to be a real asset or a real pain.

As I walked through the school's entrance, I noticed all of the posters that were up on the light yellow walls. Some were for an upcoming dance mixer. The last poster I spotted was for the Battle of the Bands. It had a grand prize of $500. Boy, did I pick the wrong profession. I should have learned how to play an instrument.

The biggest name on the poster was a band called Hearts Not Farts. I took out my notebook and jotted it down. It seemed interesting, I wasn't sure why. But that's how most of my cases started—with just one detail. It may go somewhere and it may not. You never know. Anyhow, it was in my notebook: a detective's best tool.

Battle of the Bands

October 31
Grand Prize: $500

Come see your favorite bands
battle for the prize!

Don't miss:

Hearts Not Farts

Plus:

The Astro-Nots

Fangs and the
Clawed Paws

Suddenly a crowd running down the hall pushed me. They were all screaming in excitement. I decided to check it out. They were gathered around another fourth grade kid—just a simple kid. Well, maybe he wasn't simple. He had long, greasy hair that looked like it was supposed to be messy. His clothes were, well, like a pirate costume: tight pants and billowy white shirt. He was also wearing sunglasses—inside. Man, this kid was *dangerous*. He was taking CD cases from students and autographing them. *Who was he?*

Then out of nowhere, a kid with slicked hair and a cell phone earpiece came up behind the pirate boy and grabbed him by the arm.

"All right. All right, give Mr. Blues some room," he said, pushing past the field of students. "He will be autographing copies of the new album after the Battle of the Bands tomorrow."

"What's the new album called?" a wild fan asked. She was wearing an "I ♥ Hearts Not Farts" T-shirt.

Jimmy Blues took off his sunglasses. He looked deep in the fan's eyes. He was so mesmerizing even I was entranced.

"Cheese: The Final Cutting," he said in a British accent.

The fan fainted at the last syllable. I rolled my eyes at Mr. Blues's unbelievably fake accent. As a person who watches a lot of British detective shows, I could spot a fake accent from a mile away. Mr. Blues put his sunglasses back on and was pulled away. The crowd followed him, leaving me alone—or so I thought.

"Hey, it's that kid, Dumpyshoes or somethin'," I heard a voice say from behind me. "Hey, kid, aren't you that weirdo detective from Edwin West? Yeah, yeah, I think it's him. He got my friend Donny Holiday in trouble. Now he's grounded for at least the rest of the year. Hey, kid. Come here, I want to have a few words with you."

I turned around to see who it was. It was Teddy Plugg, a fifth grader. For an eleven-year-old he looked like he had been hitting the weight room for thirteen years. He was too old to know who any of the fourth graders were. I chalked that up to an advantage and I acted fast.

"Where? I heard that kid is a total creep. He got my kid brother in trouble, too. If I ever see him, I'll show him what's for," I said, balling up my fists and pounding them into each other.

"So wait, you aren't Dumpyshoes?" Teddy asked, squinting to make sure. "I'm pretty sure you are."

"Nope," I said, with a chuckle. "My name is Frankie Flats. I've been here at Edwin East since kindergarten. I've just flown under the radar, if you catch my drift. I think Dumpyshoes just went to room 205 for his science class. I saw him walking that way."

Teddy thought about it for half a minute and rubbed the back of his head. "I guess you're right." He nudged one of the goons surrounding him and squinted a little closer. "I think I remember this jerk from around school." He looked back over at me. "Sorry, kid, didn't mean to mix you up for another loser."

I laughed, "You'd be surprised how often that happens."

"Sure thing, kid," he said. Then Teddy and his goons walked away.

CHAPTER 3
Principal Ant

As I walked to class, I heard, "Excuse me, Jon? Or is it Frankie?" It was Principal Ant. "Can I have a word with you briefly before class, please?"

I looked at his office door and then down the hallway to my classroom.

"Sure, Principal Ant. I'd hate to be late to class, though," I said.

"This will only take a minute. I'll make sure you get to class on time," he said, putting his hand on my shoulder and guiding me into his office.

I don't know what it is about principals' offices, but they all look the same to me. One corner has a filing cabinet and another corner has a college diploma. And in a third corner is an inflatable punching clown. They must come with every adult's office.

Principal Ant found his seat behind his desk as I found mine in the front. His cheeks were round and rosy. His bright red, button-down shirt was a size too small for him. And his hair was something else. I think it was a rug. It was dark brown and went down to his shoulders.

"I just wanted to take this time to see how you are doing," Principal Ant said. "How are you feeling about being here at Edwin East?"

I could not stop looking at the piece resting on his head.

"Jon?" he asked.

Then I snapped out of it.

"Hmm? Oh. It's fine, I guess," I said. "I don't have a whole lot to report. I haven't had too much trouble keeping up with homework or anything."

"Well that's great to hear," he said with both hands in the air. "There is one thing that bothers me, though. I overheard you using a false name with another student, Teddy Plugg. Is there something you want to tell me?"

"Yes, I used another name with Teddy," I said, looking over at the inflatable clown. "Frankie is my middle name. I usually go by Frankie with schoolmates. Everyone else calls me Jon."

Ant flipped through a brown file folder. "It says here in your file that your middle name is Nicholas."

I thought for a second and said, "Frankie is short for Nicholas?"

Ant pushed himself from his desk and got up. "All right, Gummyshoes. I'll buy it for now but not for long," he said. "Just keep your nose clean here at Edwin East and all will be fine. This school isn't like Edwin West. We have rules here. It's nothing like what Mr. Links is running over there."

"You know the chief?" I asked, getting up out of my chair.

Ant cleared his throat and said, "We were schoolmates a long time ago—from kindergarten through high school. That is all."

"Gee, seems like you guys have known each other for a while. Do you still keep in touch?" I asked, putting my backpack over both shoulders.

Ant brushed something off his shirt and gestured to the door with his open hand. "Just keep your nose clean, ya hear, Gummyshoes? You're going to be late for class."

And before I knew it, the door was closed behind me. Then the bell rang. Perfect, I was tardy.

Then from behind me I heard, "You're Jon Gummyshoes, aren't you?" It was the kid who was dragging Mr. Blues around.

"Sorry, pal, my name's Flats—Frankie Flats," I replied.

"Can the lies, I know Frankie Flats. He's on my Little League team," he said. "You are the famous Jon Gummyshoes. Young Frankie doesn't stop talking about you at games."

I sighed and said, "Okay, fine. You caught me. What's it to ya, huh, pal?"

"I was around the corner earlier today and saw how you handled that fifth grader, Teddy Plugg. You take care of yourself well," he said, moving a step closer to me. "I admire that."

"We all have our talents, bub," I sneered back. "Get to the point."

The kid took my hand and shook it. "My name is Blatz. Hunter Blatz," he said. "Meet me at the soccer field at lunch. I believe I have some work for you."

"What work?" I asked.

"Detective work," he responded, putting his sunglasses on and strutting off.

CHAPTER 4
A Strange Note

The bell rang at noon and I found myself walking past the cafeteria toward the boys' locker room. Fifth grade had just gotten done with gym class. The students were getting ready to rush the lunch line. It did not matter how long a fourth grader waited in line to be first. Fifth graders always cut right to the front. There was no justice in this world. I kept my eyes on the ground, avoiding the towel whips.

I opened two big steel doors that led out of the locker room to the soccer field. The sun was bright. But I could see my breath come out in streams. The frozen grass crunched with every step I took. Unfortunately, I left my jacket in my locker. I hoped that the meeting wouldn't take too long.

I approached Hunter, who was leaning up against a soccer goal with his hair still perfectly slicked over. The sun reflected off of his sunglasses, almost blinding me. It looked like he was talking to himself.

"No, no. We'll finalize the contracts at the end of the week," he said. He listened to his earpiece, laughed out loud, and put one finger up at me signaling that he needed one more second. "Yes, yes. We'll discuss it at the mini-golf course. I hope your game is better than last time. I don't know how many spare balls they can hand out." He laughed again. "Okay. Talk to you then." He touched a button on his earpiece and looked at me for a few seconds.

I waited as long as I could, and then said, "Can

we hurry this up? It's chicken-Os for lunch today and I don't want to miss it."

"I appreciate you taking time from your chicken-Os to meet me. This shouldn't take too long," Hunter said.

He reached into his coat and pulled out a green piece of paper. He unfolded it and held it out to me so I could get a good look. It was a photo of Mr. Blues. He was screaming into a microphone.

"Are you familiar with this gentleman?" he asked.

"Sure," I said. "He's the sap who's in that band—Passing Gas, or whatever."

Hunter grinned. "Hearts Not Farts—the greatest selling band of any school in the tri-county area. They perform at every school dance, county fair, and birthday party." He pointed at the picture. "This man, Mr. Gummyshoes, is Jimmy Blues. He fronts Hearts Not Farts. He is an artist who impacts a lot of people's lives."

I jammed my hands into my pockets to get a little warmth. "Okay, fine. He is a big rock star who impacts lives. What does this have to do with me?"

Hunter folded up the piece of paper and put it back in his coat pocket. "I am getting to that. Yes, he is a big rock star and an extremely talented person. This much is true. The problems I face as his manager are things not a whole lot of people know." He looked around to see if anyone could hear us and then continued. "Unfortunately, Blues is not as intelligent as everyone thinks he is. The profound lyrics that people go crazy for aren't written by him at all," he said.

"So?" I asked, losing my patience.

"So, his lack of smarts makes him a bit unreliable," Hunter told me. "I never quite see the logic behind his actions. Yes, he has the looks and he certainly has the voice. He lacks, well, he lacks the brains."

I thought about that for a second. "So you have a lead singer who's two kangaroos short of a zoo and … what? You want me to tutor him? Sorry, pal. I'm not in that business."

"No, that's not at all what I had in mind. He has a tutor, but his tutoring sessions are at Edwin West. He goes there every day after school." He pulled out another piece of paper. This one was pink. "Take a look at this, Gummyshoes. I found this in my locker this morning."

The crinkled piece of pink paper had a bunch of letters from candy wrappers cut out. The letters spelled a message: *Keep the bluebird off the stage tomorrow. Or else!* I read it and reread it. Was the note about Blues the singer?

"I'm still trying to figure out what this has to do with me," I said.

"I want you to escort Blues from Edwin West to Edwin East after his tutoring session tomorrow," Hunter said. "I also want you to figure out who sent us this threat. It seems someone is out to keep Blues from performing tomorrow. It's your job to make sure he does perform."

I chewed on the case for a second. "Why me?" I asked.

"Like I said this morning, I saw how you handled Teddy Plugg. I need a man like you. Someone who can maneuver himself past any roadblocks that are thrown his way."

"What kind of roadblocks are we talking about here?" I asked.

"There are other bands participating in the Battle of the Bands, Gummyshoes," Hunter said. "All of them have $500 in their eyes. And I feel a good number of people wouldn't mind seeing Blues not make it on stage. If you can get Blues to the Battle of the Bands and find out who sent this note, I will reward you handsomely."

I took my hands out of my pockets and started rubbing them together to warm them up. "The only reward I need is knowing the right thing has been done."

He clapped his hands together and kept them in front of him. "Great! So we have an agreement?"

I stopped rubbing my hands together and stuck one hand out. "Okay, I'll do it. I'll take the case," I said.

Hunter folded up the pink piece of paper and handed it to me. "Great, thanks, Gummyshoes. I have full faith you'll be able to solve this one in no time," he said. And like that, his earpiece was back on. He was already talking to someone else as he walked away.

CHAPTER 5

MacGuffin's Report

I went back inside and lunch was still being served. I considered walking into the cafeteria to grab a bite to eat, but I was late for a meeting. I took a right and went into the computer lab. The lights were off and no one was there. I walked down the rows of computers and found one in the way back. I booted it up and waited for it to connect. After punching a few buttons, MacGuffin was on the screen staring at me from Edwin West's computer lab.

"What took you so long?" he asked. "I have to go to class soon."

"Sorry, Mac, I got held up," I told him. "What's the news over on your end?"

MacGuffin pulled out a notebook and began reading.

"Well, it looks like Jarod O'Berry has been taken off lunchroom duty for good behavior," he said. "That could either be very good or bad for us. Let's hope he's learned the error of his ways."

"I'd say keep an eye on him," I said. "Nothing aggressive—after school details would be key. What else?"

MacGuffin looked over his notes one more time. "Nothing. Aside from that, everything is calm over here. I have to admit, Gummyshoes, you sure made this place interesting. I miss having you around." He smiled and said, "There is one more thing I kind of wanted to talk about. It's about Becky Lipgloss."

After a second I asked, "What about her?"

"She just broke up with Tommy Turner. It's all over the news. Jeff Dawkins said it was Becky who broke up with Tommy. It turns out that she's looking for a more intellectual type." He pointed at himself. "I think this might be my chance, Jon."

"Good, take this advantage," I told him. "Make sure you display your genius as much as you can, but don't flaunt it around school."

"We'll see how it goes," MacGuffin said, leaning back in his chair. "So, are you going to the Halloween party at Ice Man's tomorrow after school?"

I remembered the soccer field and Hunter Blatz. "No can do, chum. I think I have something to take care of tomorrow."

"Like what?" he asked. "Did you get a case that we can start working on?"

"Well, there is one thing," I told him. "It's sort of a bodyguard gig—for a rock star."

MacGuffin put his notebook away and zipped up his backpack. He looked back into the screen. "Which rock star?"

"Oh, that Jimmy Blues cat. The one from the fart band," I said.

His eyes widened. "Hearts Not Farts?! They are amazing! Have you ever seen them live?"

"I don't care much for live music," I said.

"What do you have to do?" he asked.

"Blues is gonna be tutored at Edwin West after school tomorrow," I told MacGuffin. "I have to pick him up and make sure he's back at East in time for the Battle of the Bands. His manager is Hunter Blatz. He knows Frankie Flats from Little League. I'm not sure about this guy, though. I'm gonna need you to do a background check for me. Ask Frankie what he knows about Hunter."

MacGuffin started writing on his hand: *Ask Frankie regarding Hunter Blatz.* "That's all?" he asked.

I stared at MacGuffin, amazed. "Mac, why do you think I bought you that notebook?"

"It's already zipped up in my backpack," he said.

I shook my head in disbelief. Then I said, "Well, it turns out Blues's manager got a threat in his locker. Someone may be planning on nabbing the lead singer before the show. Some sort of ploy to make sure Hearts Not Farts doesn't win the battle for once. At least, that's how it seems. So I'm stuck with the task of finding out who has put this plan into action and take them down."

"Take them down?" MacGuffin asked.

"Take them out. Or stop them. Whatever," I responded.

I heard the bell ring at Edwin West. Then it rang at East.

"Well, I better get going," I said.

And with a push of a button, MacGuffin was gone.

CHAPTER 6
Point A to Point B

School was easy enough the next day. Not only was it Halloween, but the upcoming Battle of the Bands had everyone crazy with excitement. Ghouls and creeps roamed the halls as I tried to get to and from class.

I took time during lunch to plan my route. Then, I did some research on this Blues character. It's amazing what you can learn from the Internet. I found something that said he was from "across the pond" but I still didn't buy that he was British. I'd figure that one out sooner or later. His favorite band was Hearts Not Farts and he didn't care much for anything else but himself. I took some notes, but there wasn't much to go on. I had a funny feeling about him, though.

I missed my computer meeting with MacGuffin. I had to connect a sidecar to my bike for Blues. After the final bell rang, I took my time getting everything else ready for the job. I pumped air into my bike tires and put a fresh coat of grease on the gears. I did an inventory of my backpack as well. I had my trusty notebook, MacGuffin's tape recorder, a flashlight, a sandwich that I made for lunch but never ate, and a copy of a *Max Hamilton* comic book for when I had to wait around. I also took a walkie-talkie that MacGuffin and I used for communication.

It got dark pretty early in October, which meant that I only had two to three hours before the sun would set. With that in mind, I glided down the street on my bicycle when school was done. I watched my breath float to the sky. Younger kids were already out trick-or-treating with their parents. Tiny princesses and cowboys ran from house to house.

I pulled up to Edwin West and realized I had some time before the tutoring session ended. I walked around the old school, remembering the good times I had there.

"Well, well, well," a boy's voice said. "Look at what the cat dragged in."

That voice always gave me the creeps. It was a voice that could only belong to a creep. I turned around and confirmed my suspicion. It was Jarod O'Berry.

"Hello, Jarod. I see you've still got your ten-gallon mouth," I said. "Lunchroom duty hasn't helped much with that."

He moved in a little closer to me. "Oh yeah, Gummyshoes? What makes you think cafeteria duty has done anything but given me wrinkly fingertips, huh?"

"I'm told you're a changed man—that you were relieved because of good behavior," I said. "Why don't you tell me what's really going on?"

He stepped back and put both hands in his pockets. "Why, sure I'm a changed person. Cleaning up the lunchroom, day after day, watching the rest of my classmates go out and enjoy the weather while I'm stuck wiping up their spilled applesauce has made me see the error of my ways." He smiled widely. "And why in the world would I want to miss the Battle of the Bands tonight?"

That clod had never been interested in music, especially if it had to do with school. "Yeah? What about it?"

His eyes lowered. "I just heard ... well, I heard this show will be quite exciting. That's all."

Something stank. I knew he was not telling me everything.

I saw an old face behind O'Berry. "All right, Jarod. School is over, you can leave now," Principal Links said, motioning his hand toward the exit.

"Sure thing, Principal Links. I was just saying howdy to my old chum. I'll be seein' ya, Dummyshoes." And like that, O'Berry was down the hall and out the doors.

Links and I stood in the hallway, staring at each other. "What are you doing here, Gummyshoes?" he asked. "I thought you were done with this school."

"I'm just doing a job. I'll be out of your hair soon, don't worry. Speaking of hair, I met your old schoolmate, Principal Ant." I could see just saying the name made Links uncomfortable. So I probed a little more. "He said you guys went to school together for a long time—all the way through high school."

"Principal Ant and I were schoolmates, yes," Links said. "We haven't spoken in a while."

"Why not?" I asked.

"You always have a question, don't you, Gummyshoes?" Links asked. "All right, Gummyshoes, what kind of job are you doing?"

"I'm on a case, but it also involves a bodyguard gig," I told him. "You have an Edwin East student who is being tutored here. I'm escorting him back to Edwin East when it's over."

Links crossed his arms. "Jimmy Blues. He's just down the hall. He will be out shortly. I expect the same from you."

"Don't sweat it, Chief," I said. "I'll be gone in no time."

"It's *Principal*, Gummyshoes," Links told me.

Links turned on his left heel and walked toward his office. I watched him enter and shut the door behind him. I turned and walked to the classroom Blues was in. I peeked through the window and saw him sitting back in his chair. He had his sunglasses on and was looking at the ceiling. The tutor was talking to the desk. The clock behind them said it was ten minutes to five p.m. Then I turned around and saw Becky Lipgloss walking down the hall.

"Ms. Lipgloss," I said, tipping my hatless head.

"Hi, Jon," she said. "What's up? I thought you were at Edwin East now."

"I am," I told Becky. "I'm just waiting for a friend is all."

"Oh? I have to admit—things are a lot quieter since you've been gone," Becky said.

"Sure, MacGuffin told me the same thing," I said. "Speaking of MacGuffin—I was supposed to speak with him today, but I missed my chance. Have you spoken with him recently?"

"Yeah, he was acting really weird today," she said. "He did a presentation on the universe, dark matter, and black holes."

"Well, see, he's quite the smarty-pants now, isn't he?" I said. "That's an attractive quality to have, if you ask me."

"The presentation was supposed to be on Europe," she said.

Darn! I told MacGuffin not to flaunt it.

"Well, anyways. I have to get going to Amber's house to get ready for Halloween," Becky told me. "So long, Jon."

"Give my best to the Holiday family, Ms. Lipgloss," I said, tipping my hatless head one more time.

"Maybe Amber and I will see you and MacGuffin at the Battle of the Bands later," Becky said.

"Sure," I responded as Becky walked away.

Then from behind me I heard, "A'rite den, mate. We goin' ta do dis, o' what den?"

I turned around and saw myself reflected in a pair of sunglasses. *His accent is so bad,* I thought.

"Mr. Blues," I said, "my name is Jon Gummyshoes. I will be escorting you from here to the Battle of the Bands. I'm parked outside. It's an easy ride—from point A to point B. Do you have everything you need?"

"Sure, sure, mate. Let's carry on whiff the proceedins den, yeah?" he said.

I stared at him for a second. "Yeah. Let's carry on, shall we?"

I took his backpack and led the way to the exit.

"Yous mates whiff dat ol' bloke, Hunter, den?" he asked me.

"No, I met him only yesterday," I said. "He said you needed assistance. I agreed to help. That's pretty much the high and low of it."

He scratched his wild hair and laughed. "Oh mate, da only person who needs assistance is dat monkey who blabbers on and on whiff his mobile. I can make it perfectly fine on me own."

"Sure, pal, I'm sure you can," I said. "But I promised your manager I'd do this. So until we get to Edwin East, you're in my sights at all times."

He stopped, took off his glasses and stared me in the eyes. "You have principles, mate. I respect dat." He put out his hand. "I want to formally introduce meself. I'm Jimmy Blues."

I stared at his hand and then shook it.

"Jon Gummyshoes," I said.

"A'rite den, Gummyshoes. Let's get a move on, yeah?" Blues told me.

We stepped outside as the sun began to slowly go down. The sky was a beautiful mix of orange, red, and a bit of pink. I was not stopped by the sight of the gorgeous sunset. But the sight of my bike stopped me. It was on its side with both tires popped. The sidecar was on the other end of the parking lot.

Standing in front of my bike were a dozen or so kids. I had no idea who most of them were, though, because they were in their costumes.

"Gummyshoes," said the one in front of the mob. He was wearing a spaceman suit and hitting a bat into his open palm. "We'd like to have a word with you."

CHAPTER 7
Maximum Frictional Force

I looked at the mob of zombies, firemen, and space aliens. They had sour looks on their faces. I tried to lighten the mood. I picked out Jarod O'Berry, who was dressed like a lizard and making weird hissing sounds.

"Sorry, fellas, I don't have any candy on me," I said. "You have to do your trick-or-treating at people's houses."

"We're not lookin' for no candy, wise guy," said a wolf. "We want something else, see?"

"And what would that be?" I asked.

"We want Blues," said the spaceman. "Give us the singer and we'll leave you out of this."

I turned to Blues and whispered, "Do you know these guys?"

"Aye, I'd recognize deez blokes anywhere. Dey are wit other school bands," he whispered back. "Not very good ones, either."

I noticed that a green watering hose was lying between the mob and us. The nozzle was behind Blues. It connected to a sprinkler near my bike. I stepped on the hose, pinching it closed.

I turned back to the crowd and held up my hands. "Okay, fine, you can have him. If it's the singer you want, he's all yours."

"Oy, Jon!" Blues shouted. "What in the blazes are ya doin'?!"

I dropped his backpack behind me and said, "Just let me get his backpack for you guys."

As I turned around to pick it up, I quickly turned on the nozzle for the water hose and turned back around.

"Okay, here, take him," I said. "It's no sweat off of my forehead. The guy is so useless if he had a third hand he would need another pocket to put it in."

I could feel the pressure building up in the hose.

"You bloody traitor!" Blues screamed.

"Duck!" I screamed back and lifted my foot off of the hose.

An explosion of water erupted from below my bike, sending it into the air. Spaceman and the wolf ran, ducking for cover as their fellow bandmates scattered. The hose began whipping around like a wild snake, spraying water everywhere. I grabbed Blues by the sleeve of his pirate shirt and pulled him as fast as I could. Then I grabbed a tipped-over bike that belonged to one of the kids in the mob.

"Get on the seat," I yelled at Blues while getting both of my feet onto the pedals. I pedaled away as hard as my legs let me.

"After them!" I heard the spaceman scream from behind me.

From one glance over my shoulder, I saw most of the mob was getting onto their bikes. I pedaled harder. The wolf pulled up to my right and swung a golf club over my head. The spaceman came up to my left with his arms held out, trying to grab me. I squeezed both of the breaks leaving black marks on the pavement. Everyone passed us and I had to turn around. I cut left onto Staple Street and pulled the walkie-talkie from my backpack.

"Mac! Mac! Are you there?!" I cried into the receiver.

"Yep, 10-4, Gummyshoes. You've got MacGuffin," he replied.

"I'm in a big pickle, Mac," I said. "Blues and I are being chased by a group of angry musicians. We're on the same bike and can't get away fast enough."

"No problem. All you need to do is find a big hill to go down. Your speed will pick up because of the extra weight giving you maximum frictional force. You'll leave everyone in the dust."

"Gee whiz, you've turned into a real genius overnight for Lipgloss, haven't ya?" I said.

"I'll meet you at Ice Man's after you lose them. Then we can figure this out," he said.

"10-4, good buddy. Over and out," I said, putting the walkie-talkie back onto my belt.

"Well, what do we bloody do now?" Blues asked from behind me.

I saw the kind of hill MacGuffin was talking about. It went straight down.

"We have to take this hill. We'll get maxim fiction forts," I said, pedaling faster.

We hit the hill after a few seconds. The wind was blinding and deafening. I squinted, trying to keep the handlebars straight. The wheels were making a solid hum. Spaceman and the rest of his flunkies tried to gain on us. It was no use, though, as we picked up more and more speed going down the giant hill.

We reached the bottom of the hill and I didn't have to pedal anymore because of how fast we were going. I made the first right turn without the mob seeing me and hopped off the bike. I grabbed Blues by the shirt and dragged him into the alley behind Ice Man's.

We hid behind a trash can and waited. After a few seconds, we saw the mob of angry musicians bike past the alley. They saw our bike and looked around. The spaceman and the wolf walked into the alley. I gripped the trash can hard and waited for them to find us. Out of nowhere, the back entrance to Ice Man's opened and I heard a familiar voice.

"Are you looking for Jimmy Blues?" he said.

"Mind your own business, pal. This doesn't concern you," the wolf responded.

"Well, I saw him and another dopey looking kid running down Jugg Street," the voice said. "They ran past Ice Man's heading east."

There was no response, but I heard feet

running out of the alley. After a second I saw MacGuffin's head peek over the trash can. He smiled widely.

"That should take care of them for a while," he said. "Let's get inside. Ice Man is throwing the Halloween party right now."

"A dopey looking kid, MacGuffin?" I asked.

He shrugged his shoulders, looked over at Blues, and said, "Mr. Blues, I just want to say that I am a giant fan of yours."

"A'rite den," Blues said. "Were you the chap who came up whiff the maxim fiction plan? Bloody good, ol' man!"

I picked up both of our backpacks, marched into Ice Man's, and said, "Right. Let's figure out how we're smuggling you into Edwin East."

CHAPTER 8
Inside Ice Man's

MacGuffin, Blues, and I pushed our way through more ghouls and goblins in Ice Man's. There was a pre-trick-or-treating party being held. We passed the arcade and pushed open the door marked "ICE MAN ONLY."

I took a moment to gather my thoughts. Then I pulled out my notebook. I checked out the clues and questions I had about the case. I still didn't know who sent that note. And I had my suspicions about Hunter as well. Then I said, "Do we have any idea who was chasing us?"

Blues took off his sunglasses and said, "Sure, mate. The spaceman is the lead singer of the band The Astro-Nots. It is a hokey band dat plays a fusion of space and punk music. The wolf is the lead in the band Fangs and the Clawed Paws—some country rap thing. I don't know, ain't me cup o' tea."

"Okay. It is apparent, Blues, that these bands don't want you to be at the Battle of the Bands. They think they will lose to Hearts Not Farts." I thought about that for a second and said, "No, that seems a little too simple."

I walked over and sat on a stack of sugar bags. "Hunter said that nobody but himself, you, me, and the teacher knew that you were being tutored at Edwin West. So one of us four must have tipped off the other bands as to where we were going to be and when."

I opened up the door and scanned the crowd. The other band members were nowhere to be seen. So I closed the door behind me.

"Well, I'd say the coast is clear. The other

bands should be pretty far from Ice Man's by now. So what we have to do is figure out how to get you into Edwin East," I said, looking at Blues.

"We better make it quick, den, mate," Blues said. "Everybody and der mums will be at this concert. And we don't want to disappoint anyone."

"I know," I said. "With all of the flyers out there it'd be hard to imagine anyone in the world not knowing about this. Who does your band's marketing?" I asked, sitting back down on the stack of sugar bags.

"Hunter himself mate!" Blues said. "He makes all of the flyers and pastes them where everyone can see."

"Well, we have a promise to keep then. We gotta get moving if we want to get you on that stage on time. I wish we could somehow pretend that you weren't Jimmy Blues and we'd have no problem." I let out a long sigh. "But pretending won't do us any good now will it, Mac?"

"You said it. I can't do it anymore! Pretending to be a genius for Becky Lipgloss hasn't helped one bit. That's one thing I've learned for sure," said MacGuffin. "I'm killing myself doing research all night just so I can sound like I'm smart the next day."

"I sometimes feel like that, too, mate," Blues said. "Hunter makes me pretend all the time. He writes the music and makes me perform, like a puppet."

"Speaking of which," I said cutting Blues off. "Mac, any word about Hunter that I should know?"

"Nothing useful, really. Frankie said Hunter couldn't hit a barn with a baseball if he were on the inside, with the door closed—whatever that means. But he also said he was sly as a fox when it came to stealing bases." MacGuffin put away his notebook. "So take that for what it's worth."

CHAPTER 9

Taking the Mask Off

We made our plan and got Blues to just outside the school. Then Blues and I had to wait—inside the Dumpster. The view from inside Edwin East's Dumpster wasn't as charming as you'd think it would be. It was a mixed salad of apple cores, old assignments, and a broken chair.

The sun was going down, so it was getting hard to see. Blues and I peeked out of the Dumpster and saw the other costumed band members in a crowd waiting for us. On the other side of the school, we saw MacGuffin holding a bag and sprinting out of the principal's office. He quietly came over to the Dumpster.

"Great, good work, Mac," I responded. I grabbed the bag from MacGuffin. "Were the supplies hard to get?"

"No. Principal Ant was taking care of things in the auditorium, so I had the office to myself," he said.

He saw me pull the contents out of the bag.

"And how are we going to get into the school?" Blues asked. "Those other band members are circling the front right now."

"With a little pretending, Mr. Blues," I replied.

I crawled out of the Dumpster, got on the bike, and headed for the mob. I quickly got their attention. I rounded the corner of the parking lot and sped through the basketball court. I looked past the body sitting on my bike to see that the angry mob was following me. I pedaled harder.

When I made another sharp left around the

corner, I was greeted with O'Berry's grinning mug. He was covered in leaves and brush. I swerved, trying to avoid him, and hit a sandbox. I went flying in the air and tumbled through the sand. I raised my head to see that the band of goons was approaching. Spaceman and O'Berry laughed at me in the sand.

"This wasn't how it was supposed to happen," I said in a weak voice.

O'Berry walked over to the body lying on the ground.

"Looks like the curtain is closed on you, pal," O'Berry said.

He nudged the body with his foot, only to realize that there was no weight to it. O'Berry bent down and flipped the body over. It was the inflatable clown from Principal Ant's office with Ant's spare rug on its head—just as I ordered.

I got up, brushed myself off, and got a piece of gum out of my pocket. Chewing gum helps me think.

"Boys, looks like you lost something," I said.

I pulled the gum out of the wrapper, examined it, and wiped some sand off on my T-shirt.

"Or should I say some*one*?" I asked as I popped the gum in my mouth.

The mob turned around to see Blues and MacGuffin running into the school. The mob ran toward them and I took my time following after. It was nice not having people on my tail for once. I breathed in the fresh fall air and made my way into the school.

I was just opening the door of the school, when I saw a flyer taped to the brick wall. I wasn't going to give it a second thought until something caught my eye. The flyer was for the Battle of the Bands. "Featuring: Hearts Not Farts," it said. This was not shocking to me. The letters that formed the words—the letters that were cut straight from candy bar wrappers— well, that was a different story. I grabbed the flyer and stuffed it into my pocket.

By the time I got inside, the performance had already started. I could hear music blaring down the halls. I got to the auditorium and saw Hearts Not Farts up on stage. But Blues wasn't singing. It was Hunter. I saw Blues standing against the wall with MacGuffin and Teddy. Beside them were the thugs who had chased us.

I have to admit, Hunter was a pretty good singer—and a liar and a cheat. I grabbed Blues by the sleeve and dragged him to the stage. Hunter saw us and I smiled at him. It stopped him from singing, but the band kept on playing.

"Hey, wait a minute, you can't be up here," Hunter said, looking at me and then to the audience. "Principal Ant, they can't be up here during a performance! Tell Jon Gummyshoes to get off the stage."

The audience gasped when they learned who I was. So I grabbed the microphone to talk some sense.

"Okay, that's right. It's me, Jon Gummyshoes,"

I said. "I took this case because it was in my heart to see that the right thing was done. Hunter asked me to make sure that his star, Jimmy Blues, made it onstage in time for the Battle of the Bands. And I did just that."

I looked over at Blues and then to Hunter. "But that's not what you really wanted, was it, Hunter? That was just to make people think you were trying to protect Blues. Then you tipped off all of the local rival bands to where Blues and I would be, down to the very time we'd be walking out of Edwin West. You knew I would protect Blues so that would give you time to make everyone believe he wasn't showing up."

The crowd gasped.

"This is silly! I took over for Blues because you couldn't fulfill your duty as a detective! Someone put that threat in my locker and you didn't even find out who it was," Hunter exclaimed.

"Ah, well, this is where you're wrong. For, you see...," I said as I pulled out the note that was slipped into Hunter's locker and the flyer I saw just outside. "I believe I have figured out who was planning this all along. As Blues has informed me, you do all of the band's marketing." Then I held out both pieces of paper for the crowd to examine. "Yet you couldn't find different candy bars to use for the threatening note, could you?"

The crowd let out another gasp.

Hunter fell to both knees. "It's true. I put my whole heart and soul into this band. I write, I manage, and I market. But it was Blues's band all along. He started it. It's still not fair! I should have been the star. Not that pirate!"

The crowd moved from gasps to boos.

"No, no, people! Hunter has a point!" I said. "You see, all this time I've been pretending to be someone I'm not. Like Hunter, who pretended to be happy with just managing the band, I pretended to be Frankie Flats. Sometimes it's just easier to not have to be yourself. But I've learned today that when you mask who you really are, then you don't actually know what you can be." I looked at MacGuffin. "Or if you're not necessarily a genius, you're a great person anyways."

"Or even if you're not British, you're still a great entertainer," Blues said, grabbing the microphone from me.

The crowd moved back from boos to gasps again.

"I bloody knew it," I whispered to him.

"My name is James Weisenborne. I'm from Akron, Ohio—not England. And Gummyshoes is right. It's fine for us to want to be one thing, but it's impossible to deny who you really are." He looked at Hunter, who was on the verge of tears, and handed him the microphone. "And if a star is who you want to be, then mate, that's who you are. You wrote the songs, you are Jimmy Blues—not me."

The crowd cheered as we walked off the stage

and Hearts Not Farts continued to rock the
house.

CHAPTER 10
Grounded in Reality

Blues (now just James) was right. The Fangs
and the Clawed Paws and the Astro-Nots bands
were terrible. So Hunter and Hearts Not Farts
won by a landslide. You can't deny real talent.
After the performance, James, MacGuffin, and I
walked outside and found the inflatable clown.
I set him upright and gave him a nudge on the
nose.

"So what now, Blue ... er, James?" I asked.

"Oh, I don't know. I loved the rock-and-roll

lifestyle for a while, but it became too fake and exhausting. I think I might take up being an actor. That sounds pretty grounded in reality," James punched the clown's nose.

"Sure it does," MacGuffin said, pushing the clown in another direction.

"But I'm going to relax for now," James said. "After today I'll need it. You know what they say, 'life is like a glass of milk.'"

MacGuffin looked over at me and I shrugged. I saw Principal Ant and Principal Links walk out of the school, not talking to each other.

"Gimme a second, will ya, fellas?" I asked. I ran toward the two.

"Principal Links, what are you doing here?" I asked.

"I'm one of the judges for the Battle of the Bands every year, Gummyshoes," Links responded.

"Ah," I said. "Principal Ant, I hope tonight wasn't too much trouble for you to clean up. I was trying to make it right for everyone. And hey, I even brought the two schools together somehow!" I said with a smile.

"Sure, Jon. No harm done. Hunter will be talked to about this. And the rest of the bands who caused trouble for you guys will be taken care of by their schools, too. Thank you for your assistance," Principal Ant answered.

"Yes, Gummyshoes. Well done," Links added.

"Well, from now on. I'm the man you look for when you want something done. That is a fact, let's shake on it," I said grabbing first Ant's hand and then Links's. "Now let's see you two shake."

They looked at each other for a few seconds, gave a weak shake, and then let go.

"We'll discuss this later, Jon," Principal Ant said, wiping his hand on his jacket. "I have a few things to discuss with Hunter and his parents."

Both principals walked away. I stood there, feeling the cold of fall. The case was cracked, but there would be more. There would always be